Look out for Bad Dog's next fur-raising adventure:

Bad Dog and Those Crazee Martians!

BAD DOG
and all that Hollywood
HooHah

Martin Chatterton

■SCHOLASTIC

Scholastic Children's Books,
Commonwealth House, 1-19 New Oxford Street,
London, WC1A 1NU, UK
a division of Scholastic Ltd
London ~ New York ~ Toronto ~ Sydney ~ Auckland
Mexico City ~ New Delhi ~ Hong Kong

First published by Scholastic Ltd, 2002

ISBN 0 439 99442 X

Printed and bound by Cox and Wyman Ltd, Reading, Berks

10 9 8 7 6 5 4 3

CHAPTER 1

Me and Bruce Willis

The last time I saw Bruce Willis I was giving him a big sloppy kiss, plenty of tongue, right on the mush – and, let me tell you, his breath isn't too clever. Kind of a horrible, minty, fresh sort of taste. No old meaty whiffs, no glorious odours of dead animal, no old shoes, nothing *interesting*.

Perhaps I should explain. I was only kissing the Brucemeister in a purely professional way, on Sound Stage 3 at MegaGlobal Studios, Hollywood.

We were shooting scene 45, take 6, of my latest star flick, *Cop & Dog*. Bruce was the cop.

No prizes for guessing who I was. This is me:

I don't actually have a real name. Most people just call me Bad Dog. People have been yelling that at me since I was a pup and it just kind of stuck.

Now, Bruce Willis doesn't really feature much in this story, so anyone who tuned in expecting me to dish the dirt on the vest-wearing one can simply tune out now. Apart from the fact that he occasionally let me sniff his butt, you'll find nothing of interest about Mr Willis here.

Let's go back, back through the mists of time, to when the story first began.

Back before I became … *The Most Famous Dog in Hollywood.*

This is the City Dog Pound, where all the dregs, the rejects, end up. It's a cold concrete shed divided into a hundred and four cells surrounding a filthy exercise yard. The stench of unwashed dogs is overpowering (actually, that's one of the only things that we like about the place: it's a *total* whifferama from a canine point of view).

This is my cell. Number 17.

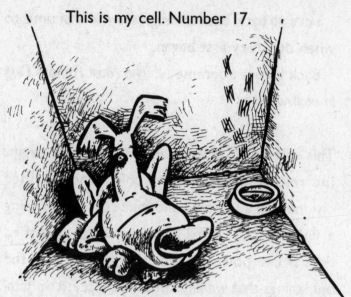

The floor is grey, the walls are grey, the door is grey. In fact, you could say the designer really went for that grey look. It's five paces wide and six paces long. Not enough room to swing a cat, really.

One thing you ought to know about me right from the start. I know it's an obvious thing for a dog to say, but I'm gonna spell it out for all you namby-pamby cat-lovers out there. Cats just make me *mad*! I see a cat, I have to chase it. And when I'm after a cat, *nothing* will stop me. You have been warned.

Z-Block, where I am, is the final home for all of us who have been "Code Sevened". A Code 7 is what they stamp on your document if you aren't needed any more. That's right, we're all on Death Row. Gettin' ready for that big lamppost in the sky. We call Z-Block the "Machine". It's a machine for turning perfectly good dogs into ash.

Of course, if you happen to be a cute Golden Cocker Spaniel you're on Easy Street. Some nice kid will come along and claim you just like that, snap, and it's a life of chasing sticks, bowls of Premium dog chow and sleeping on the couch.

For the rest of us it's Code 7 and the trip through the Green Door with Fester.

This is Fester.

He's the guy who works in Z-Block. Rumour has it that he requested a job here because he's the sort of fun guy who likes seeing dogs get snuffed.

Fester isn't his real name. His real name is Bradley Mifflin. We all call him Fester after the creepy uncle in *The Addams Family*.

None of us knows *exactly* what happens behind the Green Door. The only thing we do know is that once you go through, you don't get to come back. And those of us who are left get to move one cell nearer.

Of course, we may all be panicking for nothing. For all we know it might be Dog Heaven on the other side of the Green Door. Filthy, the resident Z-Block artist, sketched this impression of Dog Heaven to cheer us all up:

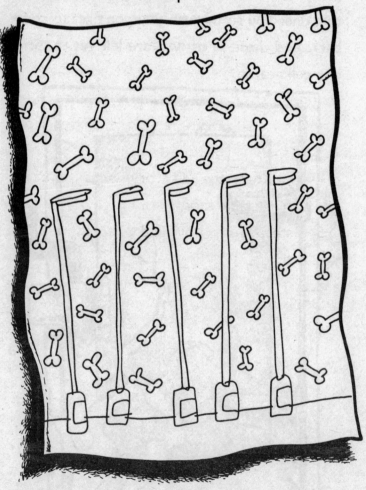

Fantastic, isn't it? But, if the truth be told, we all know that whatever is behind the Green Door, it *ain't* Dog Heaven.

I've been here six months.

I'm one cell away from finding out exactly what's behind the Green Door.

So that's everyone brought up to speed, right?

I'm a dog, sitting waiting to be turned into an ex-dog. I don't have much to look forward to, but at least I still have a sense of humour. Don't believe me? What about this...

Did you hear the sad story about the Dutch girl with inflatable shoes?

She stepped on a pin and popped her clogs. Arf! Arf!

See?

CHAPTER 2

MY LAST DAY ON EARTH

So.

This was it. D-Day. *The* Day. My last day.

"Morning, Bad Dog. Here's your slop," said Fester, carefully placing my soya bean and sawdust goop so that it oozed all over the floor and mingled with all the bits of dog hair, ticks and other unspeakable filth.

"Since this *is* your last meal an' all, I added some fillet steak and fine smoked ham just for you. Enjoy," said Fester.

Really? Maybe the kid has a heart after all. I trotted over to the bowl.

"As if!" laughed Fester. "You get the regular slop, like all the other filthy hairballs in here. No point wasting good food on you. This is the Big One, mutt. The day when you get to go through the door." Fester gave a sort of snot-filled snort.

"You know, Brad-*ley*, you are sooo attractive."

I liked throwing back witty one-liners at Fester, but today that was the best I could do. In any case he couldn't understand – I'm a dog, remember? All he could hear was a lot of barking noises.

"You keep yappin', ya dumb dog. You got till twelve and then it's *arrivederci poocherooni*."

"Poocherooni"? *Puh*-lease.

Four hours to go.

I had to face facts. I was a goner. I noticed that all the other guys on the Block had stopped talking. The ones nearest to me, Prince and Snowy, couldn't look me in the eye.

Somewhere down the hall someone started playing a harmonica. I gotta tell ya, I was choked. And not because my collar was a size too small. I settled down and waited for The End.

Suddenly there was a big commotion. I could hear voices, doors opening and the clack of expensive shoe leather on bare concrete. All the new dogs began yapping pathetically. They thought there was still a chance. Suckers.

I looked down the aisle and saw a group of people dressed all in black and wearing shades. A possible last-minute reprieve? I perked up for a second or two and then remembered the previous two thousand four hundred and sixty-two visitors who hadn't picked me. I decided to keep my dignity and ignore them.

There were three of them, plus Fester. The short, round guy at the front had a cashmere coat draped around his shoulders. Small black sunglasses sat on his large hooter. A cigar jutted from his mouth, which was surrounded by a neatly trimmed goatee beard. He was bald on top, but behind his head he had a thick, shiny, pony-tail.

There was another guy behind him. Tall and very thin. Wearing shades and a goatee and a pony-tail, just like a thinner version of the first guy. This one was holding his nose and looking like he'd just bitten into a lemon. The third person was a woman. Tall, bright-red lipstick, long blonde hair, long legs, all the curvy bits in the right places. As they got closer I could see Fester's eyeballs popping as he goggled at her. They moved down the aisle looking at all the dogs.

"No. No. No…
No. Nope. Nah,
uh-huh, no. No.
Nooooo. Too big.

Too small.

Too cute, no.

That one's got a weird
leg. Nope.

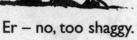

Er – no, too shaggy.

No, too skinny…"

It was obvious that these guys were real choosy. They had given the thumbs down to the pick of our little ratpack so I settled back; it wasn't going to be my day.

"This is Bad Dog," sneered Fester.

"Bad Dog?" said the tall, thin one. "Doesn't sound too good, Vince."

I took a real quick dislike to him.

"What's the matter with him?" asked Vince, the smallest and roundest of the humans. "Why's he lying down? All the others have been going bananas."

I shot him a *look*. "What do you expect?" I snapped. "You aren't going to pick me, you revolting-looking piece of human goop, are you?"

21

Then he said something that I hadn't expected. "Pity, I kinda liked the look of this one."

He what? He likes me?

All thoughts of playing dumb vanished in a split sec. And Vince? Let me scratch all that human goop stuff right here, right now. You are just about the best looking two-legger I have ever clapped eyes on. If I wasn't a guy (and a dog) I would marry you on the spot.

I played it very cool.

"TAKE MEEEEEEEEEEEEEEEEEEEEEEEEEEEEE!!!!! Takemetakemetakemetakemetakemetakemetake metakemetakemetakemetakemetakemetakeme!!! TAKE MEEEEEEEEEEEEEEEEEEEEEEEEEEEEE!!!!! Please, pretty please, please with sprinkles, strawberry sauce and little bits of nutty stuff on the top!!! PLEAAAASE!!!"

Like I said, very cool.

Of course they didn't hear any of that. What came out to them was: "RAAAAWLLLFFFFF!!!! Wooof bark rowf woof bark rowf woof bark!!! BAAAARRRRKKKKK!!!! Grrrowffff!!!"

22

I was also bouncing
off the ceiling,

doing cartwheels,

picking my bowl up

and playing frisbee with it.

If I'd had a pack of cards,
I'd have done tricks.

I grinned. I smiled. I looked like a toothpaste ad for dogs.

"Why's he doin' that teeth thing? He looks loony to me," said Vince.

What? Don't like the teeth? No problem, oh mighty one, I'll do the calm thing. Anything you like. Just TAKE ME. I sat down, stock-still, with a simpering grin fixed to my mush.

"He seems OK now, Vince. And Anvil did say to get him something very soon or he will be *very* unhappy," said the woman.

"OK, OK," said Vince. "Lemme think for a minute."

"PPLLLLEEEEEEAAAAAAASSSSSSSSSSSE!!!!!!" said a voice in my head. Every hair on my body (and there are lots of 'em) stood to attention as I waited for the verdict. Time stopped. The Earth stopped turning. Birds froze in mid-air.

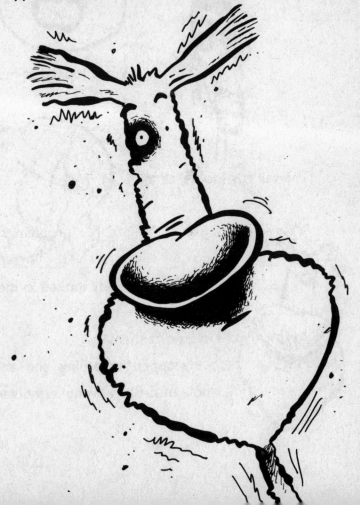

Fester looked at me.

Vince looked at me.

The tall guy looked at me.

The cute lady looked at me.

I looked at them.

I stopped breathing and the whole of Z-Block went very quiet.

"OK," said Vince. "We'll take him."

YESSSSS!!!!!

"Close that fly-trap mush, Fester, and EAT MY BUTT! I'm outta here. I'm gone! GONE! C'mon Vince, let's go, boss. See ya!" I yelped, pawing at the chicken-wire on my cell door.

Fester could hardly believe his bad luck and started to make up some goombah story about why I couldn't go. He'd obviously been looking forward to our trip through the Green Door.

Vince, who I was really beginning to like a lot, produced a thick wad of notes.

Fester produced a big bunch of keys. "Of course, Mr Gold. Right away, Mr Gold. All yours, Mr Gold. Thank you, Mr Gold. This way, Mr Gold," he drooled, his zits gleaming sweatily at the thought of being able to trouser at least some of the cash he was clutching.

Isn't money wonderful?

At last the cell door swung open, and with one bound I was free!

CHAPTER 3

HOORAY FOR HOLLYWOOD

Ten minutes later I was in the back of Vince Gold's chauffeur-driven limo as we glided through the streets of the city. I had my feet, all four of 'em, up on the smooth, tan leather seats. No one told me to get off the furniture.

Vince sat next to me, produced a huge cigar and introduced everyone.

29

The tall guy's name was Raoul ("Rah-ool") DeCinque ("Dee-sank") and the cute lady was Devon Spatula ("Dee-vawn Spat-oolar"). Raoul was Senior Acting Vice-President of Monster Flicks and for some reason he didn't seem to like me one little bit. It could have been something to do with me sitting in his seat. Vince Gold had told him to "Shift, pronto, so I can talk to my new homeboy." Raoul had shot me a look that could have cut concrete, and was now sitting in a far corner of the limo, snarling quietly into a tiny cellphone which was curled around his ear on a stalk. A quick look at his expensive-looking shoes told me he had also stepped in something nasty back in Z-Block, but I didn't want to make things any worse between us so I kept quiet. I figured he'd find out soon enough.

From time to time I picked up snatches of Raoul's phone call. He was talking to someone called Froob and he didn't sound happy. All my super-doggy hearing picked up were the words "stinking dog", "mutt", "fleabag" and "meat grinder". I looked away and concentrated on Vince and Devon. Vince hadn't mentioned what Devon did. She just sat close to him and tickled the top of his bald head. Which was easy for her as she was a clear half-a-metre taller than the little guy with the big cigar.

"Light me," said Vince.

Instantly, Raoul and Devon whipped out tiny little silver lighters. Vince looked from one to the other before settling on Devon's. Raoul sank back into his seat scowling at Devon. She gave him a nice little smile. The kind of smile that can freeze burning coal.

"Bad Dog," said Vince, leaning foward a little. "Here's the deal." Vince talked to me as if he knew I understood everything he was saying. Maybe he just liked the sound of his own voice. "We work in the movies."

"Hey, you *are* The Movies, Mr Gold," said Raoul, with a kind of sick-making simper.

"Right, whatever," said Vince, not looking up. "Now the thing is, we got a big flick stuck in casting. Casting is when we decide who plays what part in the movie. I'm an agent—"

"Hey, you are *the* agent, Mr Gold," said Raoul.

You had to give Raoul credit. He didn't quit easy.

"Stop the car," said Vince. "Get out," he said pointing at Raoul. "You can walk back."

Raoul sniggered and looked at Vince with a disbelieving look on his kisser.

"I ain't kiddin'," said Vince, opening the door. "Out."

Raoul slid out, a wounded expression on his face. The door slammed and we moved off. I jumped up to look out of the back window. Raoul stood on the baking, dusty kerb looking like he'd been beamed down from an alien spaceship. There seemed to have been a small war going on in this part of town. Most of the buildings were falling down, windows were broken, there were burn marks here and there on the walls.

A group of raggedy guys emerged from one of the broken-down buildings and began to move towards Raoul. They began to feel the sleeves of his expensive Hugo Boss jacket. He clutched his cellphone like a drowning sailor clutches a piece of driftwood and gave the limo a last vicious glance. Raoul looked right at me. He made a gun shape with his hand, pointed it at me and mouthed the word "Bang". As we accelerated away from the kerb I got the feeling that me and Raoul had plenty of unfinished business.

Back in the air-conditioned luxury of the limo, my new boss was still talking. "OK, where was I? Oh yeah, agent. I'm an agent. I'm a big agent. The biggest, in fact. The picture we're working on at the moment is ready to roll. The main star is one of the biggest movie stars in the world, Anvil Studminder. You know his stuff? Shoot-'em-ups mostly, dim comedies, that kind of thing. Great guy, great guy. Most of the other parts are being played by actors on my books. The only thing is we need to find one more part."

He eyed me carefully and smiled. "We need a dog."

Dog?

I can do dog. No problem. Woof. See? I sat up, paws in the air, then dropped to the limo floor and played dead for a few seconds. I would have fetched a stick for him, or warned the sheriff that little Ricky was trapped in the old mineshaft, but I thought that might have been going too far.

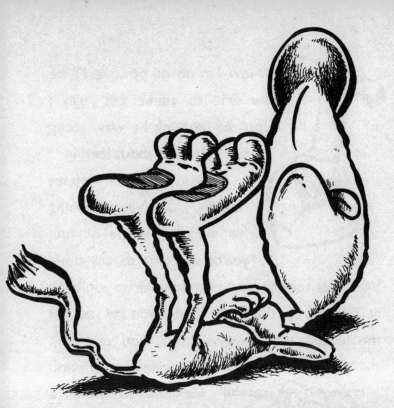

Vince carried on. "Now, we checked out all the dog actors we got on the books. All professionals, all with union cards, every one of 'em keen to do the part. The problem is, Anvil didn't like any of them. He was real specific. He didn't want any of the usual cute dogs you see all the time, Lassie, the 101 goddam Dalmatians. He wanted reality, honesty, grit." Vince hesitated for a heartbeat. "And ugly."

Now, I'm no oil painting, I'll be the first to admit, but "ugly"? Who did he think he was talking to? I thought about leaving.

"If you're thinking about leaving," said Vince, jabbing his smoking stogie at me, "you're welcome to, any time. We'll just turn the car round and drop you back at Z-Block. On the other hand, if you say yes, and the leading man says yes, then you can look forward to a life of luxury and stardom." He waved a contract at me to emphasize the point.

Hmmmm? Let me see. Say no and get dragged through the Green Door to be clubbed, poisoned and killed?

Or yes and live in a swanky pad with lackeys, pool, Roller, the whole shebang?

Difficult choice.

I grabbed the contract so fast it left friction burns on Vince's chubby fingers.

"Wolwff?" I barked. Which loosely translates as: "Where do I sign?"

CHAPTER 4

THE WORLD
ACCORDING TO ANVIL

The sound of Vince's voice faded inside my head as Vince, Devon and me swept through the gates of Anvil Studminder's (*Anvil Studminder!*) Beverly Hills mansion. Once inside the gates I goggled at what I saw. Royal palms lined the mile-long drive, at the top of which a gigantic fountain seemed to be using most of Southern California's water supply. The limo crunched over the white gravel and came to a halt outside the front door, right next to a massive olive-green army vehicle. I jumped past Devon and raced over, cocked a leg and did what a dog's gotta do against the giant wheel. It had been a long trip.

"That's Anvil's Humvee," said Vince. "They usually use them in wars. Anvil takes his shopping."

Devon's ears pricked up a little at the mention of shopping. "We goin' shoppin', Vincey babee?" she squealed.

"Course not," snapped Vince. "And it's 'Mr Gold' when we are meeting clients, so can it with that 'Vincey babee' stuff, got it?"

Devon moulded her bright-red lips into a pout. Vince rolled his eyes and carried on walking to the door.

The front door was the sort of door you see creaking open to let stranded travellers into Count Dracula's castle. Big. Heavy. Sort of scary. I began to regret using the owner's car as a toilet.

Vince clipped a gold-chain lead on to my collar. "Let's create the right impression, hey, Bad Dog?" he whispered.

As we approached the door it swung open and a small, well-dressed man peered up at us. "Good morning, Mr Gold. Mr S is expecting you. Please follow me."

We trotted into the enormous hallway. My paws slithered around on the glossy surface as I padded after Vince.

You could have taken a plane for a spin in there. I'm certain that clouds were forming somewhere up near the ceiling. Whoever lived here had plenty of cash and liked spreading it around.

I decided that it would definitely be worth my while to try and get on this guy's good side.

"Wait here, please," said the guy who had opened the door for us. He glided silently away.

As we waited in the hall, my super-doggy sense of hearing picked something up ... a dull, low rumble. And it was getting nearer.

The marble floor shook and what looked like a very expensive vase wobbled on its plinth.

Vince fiddled with his tie and looked a little nervous. Devon clutched his arm.

Suddenly, with an ear-splitting boom, the far wall erupted in an explosion of brick, plaster and paint. Paintings and ornaments smashed to the floor and enveloped us in a great cloud of dust. Vince Gold threw Devon to the floor and, by using her as a trampoline, managed to leap on to some velvet curtains and clamber to safety. I was impressed by how fast he could move.

As the dust cleared, I moved away from the puddle of panic petrol I had made on the floor and peered at the huge, metallic shape now sitting in the middle of Mr S's hallway.

It was a tank. A real one.

The hatch on top of the tank swung open, sending a shower of bricks and dust to the floor.

A figure clambered out.

It looked like this:

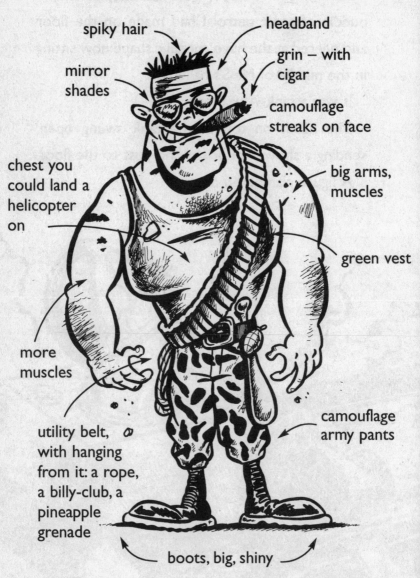

spiky hair

headband

mirror shades

grin — with cigar

camouflage streaks on face

chest you could land a helicopter on

big arms, muscles

green vest

more muscles

utility belt, with hanging from it: a rope, a billy-club, a pineapple grenade

camouflage army pants

boots, big, shiny

"Hur, hur hur!" it said. "I scared you pretty good Vincent, yes? Hur, hur, hur! This is good joke."

Vince looked down from above the pelmet, a good ten metres above the floor. "Anvil, you old son of a gun! You are a regular bundle of laffs, aren't you?" he croaked. "You kill me, you really do." He shinned down the curtain fast, skilfully cushioning his fall by landing on Devon's rear end. She was still lying on the floor, dazed and confused.

Anvil Studminder, Hollywood superstar and ex Mr Universal, had climbed down from the tank. He slapped the top of its caterpillar tread. "This is Penetrator Class Mark 3, twin-calibrated, multi-fire, nuclear-powered US Government all-terrain combat vehicle vit internal ground radar early varning system, rocket launcher, CD, leather upholstery, aircon, ABS and passenger-side air bags! She is my new baby. Still running her in. Vat do you think?"

"It — she's just great, Anv," said Vince fixing his best oily smile back on. "Plenty of leg room?"

Anvil Studminder lowered the anti-personnel rocket from his shoulder (Oh, sorry. Didn't I mention he'd been carrying one of those?) and slapped a meaty hand on to Vince's shoulder.

"Let's get down to business, Vincent."

We followed him through a doorway, Devon scrabbling to her feet and pasting a smile on to her dust-covered face. "I'm OK," she said, although I hadn't noticed Vince or Anvil ask her.

We found ourselves outside on the pool deck. The pool was big, but I was getting used to the scale of stuff chez Anvil, so barely noticed what looked like a forty-metre ocean-going yacht bobbing gently at anchor at the far end.

Anvil chucked the anti-personnel rocket on to the floor. He threw off his camouflage gear and a flunkey wrapped a soft white towelling bathrobe around him. He lay on a poolside recliner while a manicurist carefully removed the tank oil and plaster from his fingernails and a masseur gently massaged his forehead.

"Well, this is the dog who's going to be the next big movie sensation, Anv," said Vince, giving me the build-up.

I smiled as best you can without lips or cheeks.

"Vhy is he doing that thing vit his teeth?" asked Anvil. "Iss he sick?"

I decided to drop the smiling technique. It wasn't my strong point, obviously.

"I don't know, Vincent," said Anvil, looking at me through his designer shades.

"He doesn't look very action movie to me. He looks too thin, too scruffy, too drippy."

First "ugly", now "drippy". This was getting a bit personal.

"Think Nick Cage. Think John Cusack. Think Gary Oldman," said Vince. "Bad Dog here has all that. He's edgy, dangerous. He's been around the block a few times."

"I'm still not sure," said the big guy. "He needs to make the audience care about him." He paused. "Like they do vit me. They laaarv me."

As I tried to stand there looking cute, I spotted something out of the corner of my eye.

A cat!

A vile, fluffy, white feline walking straight into *my* audition! Who did that moggy think it was? There it was, large as life and twice as ugly, strolling across Mr Studminder's marble tiles It looked right at me, bold as you like, and blew me a kiss!

I was almost sick there and then, and I trembled with the effort of keeping a smile on my face. Control yourself, I said to myself. It's only a cat. Don't blow this chance. Whatever you do, do NOT chase that cat. Oh, who was I kidding?

I lasted all of five seconds before springing into action. I did what a dog has to do and chased that moggy. I snarled and sprinted after it, snagging my lead around Anvil's sun lounger. As he collapsed on to the deck, I realized somewhere deep in my brain that I was probably blowing my audition, but hey! A cat, right?

As I chased after it, the moggy wheeled sharp left into the house and began to push the door shut. I was going to lose it!

Rounding the poolside wall I tripped over something on the floor. It was Anvil's anti-personnel rocket launcher! With almost super-canine strength I hoisted the device on to my shoulder, aimed at the cat, shut my eyes and pulled the release trigger. "*Hasta la vista*, moggy," I whispered.

I opened my eyes to see that far from being the flame-grilled ex-moggy I had expected, the cat was singe-free and creased up with laughter on the inside of the house. It pointed at something behind me.

I turned around slowly.

Anvil's yacht was sinking, a thick black cloud of smoke belching from the foredeck. The crew were leaping into the water clutching lifejackets.

I had fired the rocket grenade backwards. Oops. My glittering Hollywood career vanished before my eyes in a puff of smoke. Sinking the star's ten-million-dollar boat before the audition *can't* be good. I sighed and waited for the reaction from Anvil Studminder.

Vince looked at me, an expression of complete horror running across his face. "I'm so, so sorry, Anvil. Let me assure you here and now that we are fully insured against acts of individual lunacy by any of our actors, human or otherwise and that this mangy cur will never work in this to—"

Anvil held up his hand and looked at me.

Time seemed to stand still as I looked up at the man who had sent a zillion baddies (and a fair number of goodies) to a sticky, and usually gory, end. My life flashed before me. That only took a couple of seconds and, to be honest, was pretty boring. I closed my eyes and waited for him to kill me.

Suddenly Anvil leaped to his feet and brushed

the broken glass off his massive chest. "*That's the dog I vant!*" bellowed the beefy Bavarian, pointing a huge finger at me.

"Exactly what I was thinking Anv, this is just the dog for the job," said Vince, switching track with the breathtaking two-facedness of a true Hollywood shark. "You are so right, so on the money, as usual, Anv," he creeped.

I was still in shock from sinking the *Titanic*. "Does that mean I got the job?" I barked.

"You got ze job, kid," said Anvil (who obviously understood dog language).

Chapter 5

Colin, Dog of Steel

The movie I was starring in was a delicate little picture called *Cake Fear*. In *Cake Fear*, Anvil Studminder was playing a mild-mannered, retired Special Services killing-machine commando called Jack Blade, who now lived a quiet life as a baker in a little town in Wyoming.

I played his cute dog, Colin, named after Blade's army buddy who had been killed in action years earlier. The head honcho baddie-type was called

Jurgen Swine and was played by the Brit actor Nigel Blenkinsop. He had sworn undying vengeance on Jack Blade after Blade had killed his brother. You following this so far?

That mission had been Blade's last.

Now Blade was the world's fittest and most muscular baker, turning out eclairs, doughnuts and pastries for the good folk of Sleepyville.

Meanwhile, the evil head honcho villain had escaped from prison (in a big shoot-out, natch) and was busy tracking Blade down.

My character, Colin, gets kidnapped, or dognapped, by Swine. Blade must find out where the baddies are, or his beloved dog will die a terrifying death (don't forget the movie title). Blade snaps at the thought of it. Pulling on his Special Services kit, he tracks down the baddies and, using many weapons and some terrible puns, he kills all of them and rescues me. Hooray!

In my head I could picture the trailer...

"Coming this summer, Anvil Studminder is Special Agent Jack Blade! Years ago he lost the one thing he ever cared about! Baking, and a dog called Colin, saved his life.

Now someone's getting on Blade's doughnuts again and Colin's in deep doggy-doo. It's time for Blade to turn up the heat in the kitchen, and let the fear begin!!!!!!"

OK, it's not Shakespeare, I'll give you that. But it packs 'em into cinemas from Anchorage to Zanzibar and back again. Unless it's a flop. But we don't ever, ever, mention that f-word in Tinseltown.

I'm getting ahead of myself.

After the mini-war at Anvil's ranch, and the surprising outcome, Vince whisked me back to the plush headquarters of The Gold Agency. He sank into his plush leather chair and gazed briefly up at the walls covered in photographs of himself and *everyone* who was *someone* in Hollywood. His feet dangled above the thick carpet as he picked up his phone and went to work.

Raoul was sitting on a low-slung sofa in the corner, covered in dust and sweat from his long walk back to the agency. He stared at me, the way baddies in movies stare at people they are going to strap to a table and exterminate with a super-strength laser machine.

He hadn't had a good trip back. Apart from having to escape from a mob of tramps, he had had to walk eight miles back to the agency, something he was not dressed for. He hadn't been able to call a taxi because he'd had his wallet pinched along with his watch and phone. Oh, and his shoes. His feet were wrapped in toilet paper in a vain attempt to try and stop his blisters bleeding over the deep-pile cream carpet in the agency's office.

Vince glanced at Raoul, a concerned and worried look on his face. "Quit bleeding all over the shagpile!" he yelped. "Go and do something useful, you dipstick. Run along and get our new star a cappuccino."

Raoul stood and gave Vince a sickly grin. "Of course," he slimed. "I'll give him *exactly* what he needs." As he passed me he bent down and hissed, "I'm going to make it a personal mission in life to send you back to Z-Block, whatever your name is."

"The name's Bad Dog, you stick insect," I snapped back. "Don't ever forget it." Totally wasted of course. It just came out as a load of barking noises. I looked over at Devon for support, but she was just smiling vacantly. If this was a sci-fi movie she would turn out to be an android.

Raoul stalked out of the room as Vince put down the phone. He turned to me with a grin and signalled me towards a chair. I jumped up on to the white suede couch and listened. As far as I could understand, the film company was paying me half-a-million dollars for the movie.

Raoul had returned with the coffee and his mouth dropped open as he heard this. I swear that a thought bubble saying, "But that's not *fair!*" appeared above his head.

Vince explained that he would take most of that in fees. He had to pay for my lawyer (whose last name, funnily enough, was Gold), my accountant (another Mr Gold, natch) and various other gophers and dogsbodies. There was also my new image to consider, my hair-stylist, my manicurist, my personal shopper, my psychiatrist and my bodyguard ("One should do for now, eh mutt?" Vince had said. "After all, you ain't Madonna yet, are ya?").

"So … when everything has been taken into consideration," said Vince, brandishing his calculator in one chubby paw and his phone in the other, "you owe me twelve thousand dollars."

"Seems very fair to me, Mr Gold," I said. I am a dog, after all. What do I know?

So I went to stay with Vince in his swanky Beverly Hills pad. I was only renting, you understand. Vince was letting me stay there for about eighteen thousand dollars a week. But, whatever it cost, it sure beat Z-Block paws down.

CHAPTER 6

MR. BAD DOG

CAKE FEAR

My first days on the set of *Cake Fear* were an education, let me tell you.

I turned up with Vince and Devon in tow. For some reason, Raoul, who normally followed Vince around like, well, like a dog, wasn't there. He'd caught a bug, he had said. I was glad he wasn't around. He was giving me the creeps.

In addition to Vince and Devon, I also had a personal trainer (Randy) whose job was to get me to do the things needed in the script,

a personal hairdresser (Mandy),

a dietician (Andy),

a bodyguard (Sandy),

71

an assistant (Candy),

her assistant (Dandy)

and a nervous-looking
guy who sat in a
corner and ate
jelly beans. He
was my psychiatrist,
Doctor Landry.

Me, Randy, Mandy, Andy, Sandy, Candy, Dandy and Landry all had plenty of room in my super-jumbo-monster, air-conditioned kennel/trailer on the set. My trailer was right between the gigantic one belonging to Anvil Studminder and the stupendous-sized one of the leading actress, Hayley Froob. More of Froob later.

I had my fur done by Mandy, while eating a breakfast of Himalayan mongoose liver and Thai fishcakes, carefully prepared by Andy. Sandy tasted it first to check it was OK. Candy went through the script along with Dandy. Randy and Landry tried to make sure I knew what I was doing.

They were driving me *mad*.

And my cool new look, courtesy of Mandy, had some drawbacks. The gel on the top of my head felt greasy and I wasn't keen on the false specs.

"They are all the rage, BD," squeaked Mandy. "They make you look sooo intelligent." I wasn't sure, but I took her word for it.

"Right, Bad Dog, good boy, Bad Dog, who's going to be a clever ickle doggy-woggy den?" said Randy, smiling at me and giving me *big* teeth. If he'd had a piano wedged in his mouth I couldn't have seen more ivory. "In your first scene the script calls for you to carry an unexploded nuclear bomb out of the disused coal mine, saving Jack Blade's life. Let's pretend this stick is the bomb, OK? Go get the stick, Bad Dog." He threw a chocolate-coated stick a short distance over my shoulder. I looked at it.

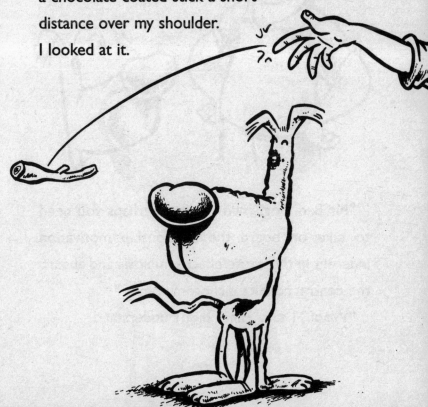

"Woof," I said, not moving a muscle. I understood everything Randy had said but after a week of prime rib-eye steak there was no way I was lowering myself to chase a mere chocolate stick. Besides, I was saving myself for the actual filming.

Randy shot me a disappointed look.

"Mr Bad Dog," said Landry. "Perhaps you need to take on board the relationship motivation inherent in this cause/effect symbiosis and absorb the central conflict dichotomy, hmm?"

"Woof," I said. *Him* I didn't understand.

There was a knock on the trailer door. Before Sandy could get to it, it swung open, and the most glamorous human being I had ever seen swept in. Tall and blonde, all cheekbones and teeth, it could only be Hayley Froob, the most famous female movie star in the world, who was playing Jack Blade's fresh-faced, clean-livin', country-gal girlfriend, Kit Gritty.

She opened her mouth and smiled. Like a T-Rex might smile. I'd heard some rumours around the set about Hayley Froob. How difficult she could be, how she ate directors and crew members for breakfast, how she insisted on her trailer being lined with Florentine marble, and on having fresh mangoes flown over from the Caribbean for her breakfast every morning. And here she was. In my trailer. "Bad Dog, dahling! I just had to come and wish you luck on your first day!" she beamed.

How nice, I thought. All those bad things I'd heard must be nonsense after all.

"And," she continued, still beaming like a maniac, "to warn you that if you do the *slightest* thing to stop *me* being the single best thing about this movie, I will crush you like a cockroach and grind your meaningless carcass into dust. Got that, fleabag?"

I managed a nod.

She turned on her shiny red heels and stepped out of the trailer, leaving a haze of expensive perfumes behind her.

Dr Landry rushed over and started counselling me. He was worried that I'd be suffering the after-effects of the brush with Froob. He needn't have bothered – I'd spent too much time on Z-Block to let a little Hollywood tantrum spoil my day. *I* was a professional.

"Call for Mr Bad Dog. Mr Bad Dog on the set, please." A metallic voice came through on the trailer intercom.

This was it. Showtime!

I stopped in front of the full-length mirror and checked out my reflection. "Mmmm-*mmm*!" I said. "Just get a load of your own bad self! You are looking baaaaad!"

I was ready to become a star!

Waiting for me on set, surrounded by cameras, crew, lights and machinery, was the director, Filch Softly.

"OK, Bad Dog," said Filch, softly. "Let's make a picture."

"Scene 36, Take 1. Roll 'em," said a skinny guy

holding up a board with writing on it.

Under the bright lights, Anvil Studminder was already on the set. He lay on the ground, pinned there by a pile of fake wooden beams. His face was gashed and he had fake blood running down his bulging muscles. A fake bomb lay next to him, slowly ticking. This was the bomb I was supposed to carry out of the mine.

"Hi, Bad Dog," said Anvil. "Velcome to the movies! Just relax, you'll do fine."

"And … ACTION!" shouted Filch Softly.

Everyone looked at me. I trotted over to the bomb and began dragging. I made it look as though the bomb was real heavy, although it was made of plastic. As I passed Anvil I noticed a nice whiff of strawberry coming from his forehead. I knew it wasn't in the script but I couldn't resist. I stopped, trotted over to him and began to lick his head. The fake blood was made of strawberry jam. My fave flave.

"Keep rollin'!" whispered Filch. "This is great!"

"The bomb, Colin ... the bomb," said Anvil through clenched teeth. "Get ... the ... bomb ... out."

I gave Anvil's head one last lick, turned around, got the "bomb" and dragged it off the set. I didn't know where to leave it so I left it under Hayley Froob's trailer. It would be safe enough there, I figured.

85

"Cut!" yelled Filch Softly, a big grin spreading across his mush. "Print it. Let's get the next scene ready, people."

Almost instantly an army of guys ripped apart the disused-mine set and began making it into the underground headquarters of the movie villain.

Anvil came across and patted my head. "Nice vork, kid. Licking my face vas a nice touch, the audience vill go big on that."

Just then I noticed Raoul standing in the shadows, on the far side of the set from the trailers, a sly smirk sitting on his face like a bad smell.

What was he so pleased about? My super-doggy senses kicked in. I was getting a bad feeling about that smirk. Wasn't Raoul supposed to be ill?

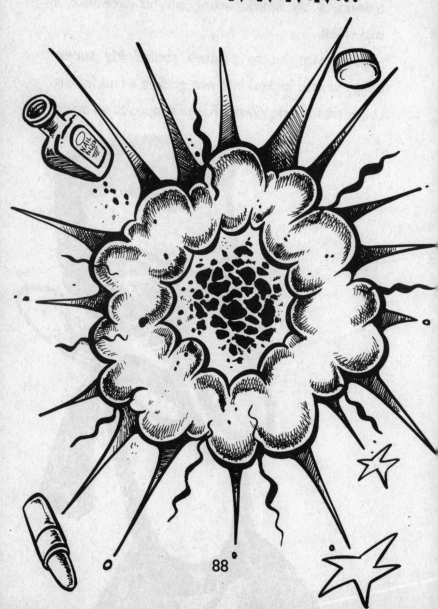

Hayley Froob's trailer exploded in a shower of sparks and smoke. Everyone screamed and dived for cover. As the smoke began to clear, the shattered door of the trailer swung open and Hayley Froob staggered out. Her designer clothes hung in smoking tatters, her face was a soot-blackened mess and her hair stood on end, the tips still burning. "I … I … who … wha…" she choked.

Before she could say anything else, three guys in firefighting uniforms stepped forward and hoisted fire extinguishers on to their shoulders. I just had time to catch a glimpse of Froob's gimlet eyes looking straight through me, before the full force of three hi-power foam extinguishers caught her square in the face. The firefighters stuck to their job. They emptied those suckers all over the world's most famous female movie star. It took a while, too. Long enough for me to realize that this didn't look good for me. By the time they had finished Froob was just a pile of foam, her eyes the only part of her still visible. A plume of black smoke rose from the top of the foam. She looked like a barbecued ice-cream sundae.

"WHO ... DID ... THIS?"

screamed the pile of foam.

In a nano-second everyone sort of backed away from me and formed a circle. Filch Softly cowered behind his chair. Anvil Studminder seemed to be coughing in a way that made me think he had been laughing. Randy, Sandy, Mandy, Candy, Dandy, Andy and Landry all tried to put as much distance between themselves and me as possible. Vince Gold looked like he was having some kind of heart trouble and Devon Spatula was fumbling for his pills. Everyone looked shocked.

Raoul, on the other hand, looked like he had won the state lottery. Twice.

"Woof," I said. I couldn't think of anything else to say.

"YOU'RE FINISHED IN THIS BUSINESS!! FINISHED!!!" yelled

Froob, pointing at me, before collapsing, sobbing, on the floor. She was immediately surrounded by gushing helpers who carried her away.

A hand tapped me on the shoulder. It was Raoul. "Strange the way that bomb went off like that, eh?" he whispered. "Almost like somebody wanted you to get the blame…" He walked away, chuckling nastily.

I had to admit, my first day could have been better. I headed back to my trailer, my tail firmly between my legs.

CHAPTER 7

i BOUNCE BACK!

In the trailer I sat thinking about what might have been. Fame, fortune, as much Bonio as I could eat. All of this was now history. I choked back a small tear of self-pity. I began to get my belongings together for the trip back to Z-Block. It wasn't much: a bit of old blanket and a rubber chew toy.

There was a knock on the door and Anvil Studminder came in.

"Hur, hur hur," laughed Anvil as he lowered

himself and his muscles into a chair. "That was ze funniest thing I haf ever seen! You are a genius! She's been due for something like that for a long time."

And that turned out to be how a lot of people felt. Hayley Froob did her best to get me off the movie but my performance in front of the cameras had convinced everyone I was worth keeping.

"It's what's up on the silver screen that counts in the end," said Filch Softly to me back on the set. "No one gives a rat's ass how you do it, as long as you do it. To be honest, I had been itching to get rid of that Froob dame since we started. She was costing this movie a bundle. Now we'll get insurance to pay her off, re-jig the script and replace her with some state-of-the-art graphics effects, right?"

I nodded and breathed a sigh of relief. Not as big as the one that Vince puffed out when he found out I was still on the movie. "See," said Vince, jabbing Raoul in the ribs, "I told you we picked a winner in this guy!"

Raoul didn't reply. He seemed to be having trouble breathing. He just stood there grinding his teeth.

The rest of the day's filming went well, once the wreckage of Hayley Froob's trailer (and the wreckage of Froob herself) had been disposed of. She had had to be dragged from the set by security after she tried to strangle anyone who came near her. Honestly, no *professionalism*, some people.

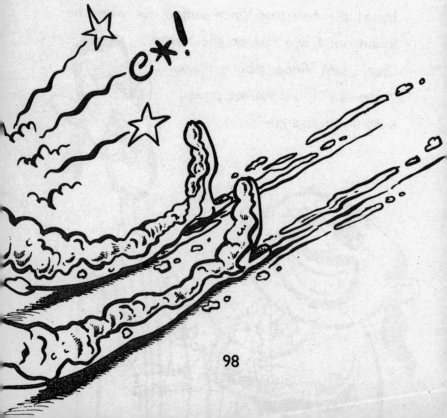

For some reason, everything *I* did seemed to be exactly what Filch wanted. In the scene with Nigel Blenkinsop, the actor playing the chief head honcho villain, I had ad-libbed a "playing dead" thing which brought the house down.

What can I say? I'm a natural.

And when Anvil had had his big fight scene with the baddie, I had joined in by biting his ankles (the baddie's, not Anvil's). Again, this went down well with everyone behind the cameras. Nigel didn't seem that impressed, though.

As we stood around waiting for the limos to take us to dinner, Filch put into words the question that had been bugging me. "Not sure why that bomb went off like that," he mused. "It was supposed to be just a prop."

"Hmmm," I said darkly, throwing Raoul a "look". I couldn't prove a thing but I knew, just *knew*, that Mr Dee-Sank had something to do with the Froob incident. I licked my butt thoughtfully. I would have to watch that guy a little more carefully.

"I knew you had the right stuff, kid," said Vince. "I knew my instincts were right. Thank God my money's – I mean – you, you're OK."

"Yes," said Raoul, standing close behind Vince and eyeing me nastily, "working in the movies can be very dangerous if you don't know exactly what you're doing." He stroked his creepy little goatee beard. It looked like a small hairy snake had wrapped itself around his chin and gone to sleep.

Dinner was … interesting.

We went to the trendiest restaurant in town. It was only because Anvil was with us that we managed to get a table.

"Of course, Mr Anvil," oiled the little manager, showing us to our seats. There were some other people there but he elbowed these ordinary people out of the way. "For you, we always find a table, Mr Studminder, sir."

The restaurant was called *Jaws* and it had a "dangerous fish" theme. One wall of the restaurant was entirely filled with a gigantic aquarium. Softly lit, sleek, grey-blue sharks slipped past the diners, just centimetres from the tables. Monster jellyfish floated near the surface. Poisonous lion-fish lurked behind rocks. A spooky black manta ray slid lazily along the bottom, past a massive conger eel. The rest of the tank was filled with various other spiny, vicious, sharp-toothed, toxic finny things. A bit like the restaurant really, I noticed, casting an eye over the motley bunch stuffing their faces.

The restaurant was filled with really really nearly famous people. There was a guy who'd been in an episode of *Friends*, and someone who said they knew someone who'd once seen Sandra Bullock's mother at the hairdressers. Quite a star-packed crowd, in fact.

Vince, Anvil, Devon, Raoul and Filch all ordered raw fish with expensive glasses of water. I had a raw steak with a side order of Bonio.

As Filch told everyone what a great find I was, Vince grinned from fat ear to fat ear. "I always knew this guy'd cut it," he said, looking at me and sliding a forkful of yellow slime into his mouth. "He's gotta great future in the business."

"I think we might be talking Best Supporting Actor Oscar material here, Vince," said Filch. "Right after Anvil picks up his Best Actor gong, eh?"

As the *Cake Fear* movie people schmoozed, Raoul pushed his chair closer to mine and started whispering in my ear. "Nice aquarium," he said, nodding at the vast tank.

"Woof," I said. I didn't want to commit myself to anything more at this stage. I noticed he had hold of a large serving tray. Strange, I thought.

"Plenty of unusual fish in there," he said, eyeing me. "Sharks, rays, lion-fish, stone-fish." He paused and leaned in close to my ear, so that only I could hear him as he whispered, "Even one or two CATFISH…"

Afterwards, witnesses said that they were aware of a blur of movement from the area near where I was sitting. Then all they remember is water, and fear, and everything going black...

What actually happened was that as Raoul said the c-word, a red mist dropped over my eyes and I peered closely at the fish he had kindly pointed out. It definitely *looked* suspiciously on the feline side: sly, nasty eyes, long, sneaky, disgusting whiskery things on its nose. As far as I was concerned, it was close enough.

I erupted from my seat with one thought on my mind. That cat was gonna get it. I raced the length of our long table towards the aquarium, upending plates of sushi and glasses of Perrier all over Anvil, Filch, Devon and Vince. As I reached maximum cat-chasing speed the cat(fish) just stared back at me. Stupid cat, I thought. Doesn't it know it's about to get creamed?

I realized why the catfish wasn't too worried about my approach just a moment too late as my head made contact with the five-centimetre-thick reinforced glass of the aquarium wall.

There was an almighty crunch as bone met glass and I bounced back on to the table. Things went blurry for a few seconds. Luckily for me, I have a very hard head surrounding a very small brain. I sat on the table and slowly looked up. There was a funny sort of groaning noise. I checked to see if it was me and it wasn't.

Then I realized.

The groaning was coming from the glass wall.

The glass wall holding nine hundred tons of water and dangerous fish.

A tiny hairline crack had formed where my head had made contact. The entire restaurant stopped and watched as a maze of cracks slowly spread out from the first point of impact. The creatures behind the glass were gathered looking at the crack, too. Some of them almost seemed to be smiling.

As the groaning grew to almost unbearable levels, the giant glass wall seemed to bow gently outwards. For a split second the noise stopped.

In the silence I had time to hear Vince Gold whimper "Mummy" before the glass shattered into a gazillion pieces.

Well, all that water had to go somewhere and it didn't waste a second in joining the rest of us in

the restaurant. The lucky few were swept out of the doors and windows on a tidal wave and deposited in the street outside. I noticed Raoul standing on the large tray he had been holding and surfing expertly out of the main entrance.

He was humming a surfing tune and talking to someone on his mobile phone. "It worked like a dream, Ms Froob," I thought I heard him say, but with all the water and glass I couldn't be sure.

Those left inside weren't doing so well. As I doggy-paddled out of the restaurant I saw some very disturbing scenes. A large, round man, the film critic for *The Hollywood Gazette*, was being eaten by one of the sharks. I heard his last words before he disappeared down the gaping maw of the Great White. "This is *soo Mission Impossible*," he shouted, "at least make it original! Two thumbs down!"

Most of the other sharks had been badly bitten by a group of Hollywood agents who, with the scent of blood in their nostrils, were now circling a nervous-looking giant squid. Anvil Studminder was doing his best to swim to safety with a ten-metre-long eel wrapped around him. Filch wasn't far behind them and neither was the two-metre barracuda who was giving chase. He would have been in trouble, but twenty years of Hollywood survival skills kicked in. He had hold of the 'cuda and was shouting, "Ya want some? Ya want some?" as he traded bites with the killer fish.

Vince Gold was using Devon as a lifeboat and speeding to safety using a dessert spoon as a paddle. By the speed he was going I'd say that fella had some white-water-rafting experience behind him. I didn't have time to see how the rest of the diners were doing. It was a dog-eat-dog world.

It was all over in a few wet minutes. As the waters went down, the fish lay gasping amongst the remains of the restaurant and the diners.

I sat up in the middle of Sunset Boulevard and spat out a lungful of salty water.

I didn't even get the catfish.

CHAPTER 8

i FOUGHT THE LAW

It took for ever for the fuss to die down (and there was a truckload of fuss, believe me). "MMMMFFFFFFFFFF! SPPPPPFFFTTTHH!! HRTH NTYGTY!!!" said the restaurant manager, an inflated Bandtail Puffer wedged spikily in his mouth. He still managed to point me out to the police, though, and I was hauled into a squad car. This was most definitely The End. Nothing could save me, or my career, now.

So I was surprised when Vince popped up next to the squad-car window with some words of encouragement.

"We'll get you a good lawyer, kid," he said, pulling a small Atlantic Torpedo Ray from inside the back of his shirt. "Say nuthin'."

Anvil strolled over, brushing bits of conger eel from his Armani. "Eel feel bad in da morning!" he quipped, sounding like one of his movies. He leaned through the car window and whispered to me, "Good vork, kid! Don't vorry about a thing."

Even Devon winked at me and gave me the thumbs up.

But Raoul, who should have been celebrating, was exploding with rage. His goatee vibrated with fury as he glared at me. What was his problem, I wondered? Surely his plan had worked a treat?

I was still puzzling over this as the whoop-whoop of the squad-car siren cut the air and we pulled off into the traffic.

I got some answers back at the Beverly Hills copshop.

"I ain't talkin', copper," I snarled at the desk sergeant. "Get me my lawyer! Please," I added, spoiling the effect a little.

But it didn't matter, because (a) he didn't speak dog, and (b) he wasn't listening. He was holding out a piece of paper, a silly, dazed grin on his face.

"Can I get your autograph?" he said.

In Hollywood, everyone, even the police, want to get into the movies. Word had spread around the station house that I was co-starring with Anvil Studminder in a new action smash, and before you could blink, every flatfoot in the building came for a gawp at the celebrity prisoner.

By the time Vince and Devon arrived with the laywer I was sipping a freshly-made pork-chop milkshake in between signing autographs. Sergeant Perez was tickling my ears.

"OK, Bad Dog, you're out," said Vince.

"But what about all the damage and injuries and all the rest of it?" I yelped.

"In case you're wondering about all the damage and injuries and all the rest of it," said Vince, "it's all been settled by the studio."

It turned out that the studio didn't mind paying for the restaurant damage, or for the injuries. Or the funerals.

Thanks to the incident at *Jaws*, *Cake Fear* and me were front-page news. And, as Vince never got tired of telling me, "There ain't no such thing as bad publicity."

Cake Fear had featured heavily in all the papers, and on the TV evening news.

"*Everyone's* gonna wanna see the dog who did all this," grinned Vince. "*Cake Fear* is gonna be a smash!"

The next day when I arrived on the set, the whole crew stopped and clapped me to my chair. I was a hero! And things carried on like that for a while.

Raoul was the only blot on the landscape as far as I was concerned. He spent a lot of time muttering into his cellphone and glaring nastily at me every chance he got.

Dr Landry had me lie down on a couch in the trailer every lunchtime to check I hadn't gone totally fruitloop. He showed me some inkblots and asked me how I got on with my mother and then said I was making good progress.

Randy, Andy, Mandy, Sandy, Candy and Dandy all did whatever it was they were supposed to do.

Vince popped in every day to check on his investment, Devon and a scowling Raoul scampering behind him.

I turned up on time, did what Filch Softly and Anvil Studminder wanted me to do (plus a bit more to keep 'em sweet) and went home to Vince's superduplex pad in the hills.

One day, after a few weeks of this, Filch turned to the crew and made an announcement.

"Can I get your attention, people?" he said, wiping a big fat tear from the side of his face. "Ladies and gentlemen, it's a wrap."

What he meant was that the film was finished.

Cake Fear was due to be released in a few months. My next movie was the one with Bruce Willis. I was shooting that one just before *Cake Fear* came out. In the meantime Vince and the studio organized a promotional tour for me and Anvil. Interviews, press, radio. And TV.

It was great. I was chauffeured from glitzy hotel to glitzy hotel while people smiled at me and asked questions. Anvil Studminder seemed to love every minute of it. He answered most of my questions as well as his (which was just as well, otherwise the interviews would have been a bit one-sided).

The only down-side was that Raoul had volunteered to come with us. I had no proof Raoul had had anything to do with the Hayley Froob explosion, or the *Jaws* aquarium disaster, but that guy made me nervous. And volunteering for this tour smelled fishy to me. Mind you, most things smelled fishy to me after the palaver at *Jaws*. There had been a number of niggly little problems on the tour. Late limos, lost hotel keys, doggy-doo turning up in Anvil's room (not mine, honest). It all looked like Raoul's work to me.

We were booked on the last appearance of the tour. The biggest live TV chat show in the country: *The Jaz Reno Show*. This one appearance would be seen by more people than we had reached in the rest of our promo tour put together. "Gazillions of bums on seats," as Vince put it. The Reno show could be make or break for *Cake Fear*.

It was the evening before the Reno show appearance. Raoul had been behaving strangely lately, smiling pleasantly at me, even, on one stomach-turning occasion, tickling my belly. He was being too nice for my liking. I wanted to know exactly what he was up to.

That evening I got my chance. I was investigating some interesting smells behind a large cheese plant in the hotel lobby when I heard Raoul's voice. Like always, he was talking fast into his little mobile phone.

I crept nearer. Near enough to overhear what he was saying.

"Yes," he whispered, "I got the stuff right here." He patted a side pocket in his jacket and fished out a small bottle. "And you're sure that this is the genuine article? I mean, I don't want to do all this if all we got here is some aftershave... OW!" He jerked the phone away from his ear like it had bitten him. Even from several metres away I could hear the tinny voice yelling at him: "WHADDYA MEAN, 'Is it genuine?' YOU ARE FREAKIN' *RIGHT* IT'S THE REAL DEAL! I COLLECTED EVERY DROP PERSONALLY, YOU JUMPED-UP LITTLE PUTZ! DO YOU HAVE *ANY* IDEA HOW DIFFICULT THAT WAS?"

There was something very familiar about that voice. I couldn't quite place it though. Yet.

"OK, OK, Hayley. I know you want this more than I do," whined Raoul, rubbing his ear.

Hayley? I thought. I *knew* I recognized that voice. *Hayley Froob!* Question was, what was Raoul DeCinque talking to Hayley Froob about?

Raoul was finishing up his conversation with Old Foamhead. "Sure, Hayley, Ms Froob, I'll get right on it. After this he'll never work in Hollywood again. I'm going over to Reno's dressing room right now. Yes. Uh-huh. Yep. Mm. Yep. OK. Catch you later, let's do lunch. Ciao." Raoul folded the phone up, slipped it into his jacket and checked his watch. He got up, looked around and started for the exit.

What did Raoul have in that bottle? And why was he going to Jay Reno's dressing room at the TV studios? He was definitely up to something. Something which included me. Back in my room, I settled down on the floor and gave my butt an extra-thoughtful lick.

CHAPTER 9

BUM RaP

I didn't have long to wait to find out what Froob and Raoul had planned.

The Reno show was going well. Jaz was wisecracking with Anvil fit to bust. I was happy enough doing my cute-pooch thing and the audience was lapping it right up. But at the back of my head there was a nagging worry. What *was* in that bottle?

I found out soon after the second commercial

break. Anvil was getting started on a long and fairly boring story I had heard a zillion times before. Suddenly Jaz Reno shifted in his chair and I got a definite waft of something. Something guaranteed to get my blood boiling in a micro second. The pong was CAT!

Reno stood up to wind up the show. The foul stench of cat became overpowering. None of the humans noticed a thing, but to me it was like having an entire nest of the evil beasts squatting in my nose.

Reno was in mid-spiel. "I'd like to thank Anvil for coming in once again to plug another movie! And of course for introducing an audience of forty million to the nicest four-legged actor working in Hollywood ... Bad Dog! What did you think of our little show, Bad Dog?"

As he spoke, the old red mist came down and I leaped to my feet. With a snarl I jumped forward and sank my fangs deep into the Reno buttocks. I knew he had had nothing to do with it but I couldn't help it. It's the way I am. As I growled and gnashed, I could see Raoul snickering on the side of the set.

Suddenly all the bits fell into place.

Everything was down to Raoul and Froob. The bomb. The catfish. And this. *All* Raoul and Froob. Raoul had sprinkled the cat wee he had been given by Froob all over Reno's pants, knowing *exactly* what my reaction would be. Forty million TV viewers watched my career vaporize as I attacked America's best-loved TV host.

Something wasn't quite right, though. Why wasn't Reno howling in pain? Reno looked around and saw me hanging off his butt, my jaws clamped around a fair portion of his tenderest bits. He didn't bat an eyelid as he turned back to camera, hands clasped, and wisecracked, "Everyone's a critic." Was this guy a robot, or what?

The studio audience cracked up. Jaz Reno waved to them and walked off stage with me still firmly clamped to his butt. As I passed Raoul he made an odd face. I swear he had a thought bubble coming from his head reading, "Curses! Foiled again!" But that might have been my imagination. He turned on his shiny Patrick Cox heels and stomped off.

As my jaws were being prized from Reno's rear end all was explained.

"We had a bad incident with a tap-dancing rottweiler a few years back," said Jaz, stepping out of his tattered pants. Underneath he had on a huge pair of dark-green Y-fronts. They were unlike any I had ever seen — thick, bulky and stiff-looking.

"That's why I always wear these whenever there's a British rock band or anything with teeth on the show." He pointed to his undies. "They're made of kevlar. The stuff they make bullet-proof vests from."

I squinted at the label. "Parkinson's Patented Pant Protectors! Guaranteed 100% Butt Bite Protection."

He chuckled and patted my head. "That ending was a riot, man! Thanks."

Rock and Roll! I can do no wrong! If I was any luckier I'd be a four-leaf clover.

With all the fallout from The Reno Bum-Biting Incident, people couldn't wait for *Cake Fear* to come out. They didn't have long to wait. Two days after we arrived back in Hollywood we were at the ritzy LA premiere at Mann's Chinese Theater on Hollywood Boulevard. I was looking forward to seeing *Cake Fear* as much as anyone, as I had only ever caught glimpses of it on set.

The limo pulled up and I stepped out of the car. The blast of camera flashes blinded me for a moment as I started up the red carpet.

Screaming fans were held back behind golden ropes. I stepped into the theater and settled down between Vince and Anvil to watch the movie.

My movie!

The opening scenes dragged by. Mainly because I wasn't in them. Up on the screen, Anvil was in the Nicaraguan jungle wearing a lot of camouflage. So were his muscles. In fact his muscles should have had a movie to themselves, they were so big.

As Jack Blade shot lots and lots of really big guns at loads and loads of bad guys, I stifled a yawn.

When Jack Blade's best friend fell off a rope to his death, Anvil gave me a nudge. "This iss my Big Acting Bit, BD!" he whispered, excitedly. "Check it out."

On screen, Anvil's Big Acting Bit came up.

The camera closed in on his face. His right eyebrow twitched and his mouth turned down about a millimetre. And then he jumped off the rope and began shooting again.

"What do you think?" said Anvil to me. "Did you like it?"

"Top eyebrow movement, man," I said.

He smiled at me and patted my head. I sometimes got the feeling that Anvil could understand everything I said.

On screen things got interesting as we cut to Sleepyville and suddenly, ten metres tall, there was ME! Personally I felt the movie really kicked into gear now the main dog had arrived.

There was one embarrassing scene where I tried to cheer Jack Blade up by rolling in flour, licking his hand and doing a lot of other very cute doggy things. If any other dog had done what I was doing up on screen, I'd have reached for the sick bag, pronto. *And* filled it.

But the audience didn't agree with me. "Aaaaaaaaaaaahhhhhhhhh!" they smiled, putting their heads on one side and nudging one another. They loved it.

Vince reached over and there was a gleam in his eye. "Hear that, kid? That's the sound of money! Money coming to *me*. I mean us," he added hastily.

I began to swell with pride. I *was* a star! I mean, I was really good at this stuff!

As the credits rolled, Filch Softly made his way to the stage. "Ladies, gentlemen and dogs. Thank you for being the first ever audience for *Cake Fear*. I hope you agree with me that it's the greatest movie ever made, and that I am a godlike genius. Many people gave a lot to make this motion picture. The studio gave Anvil forty million dollars, for example. But there is one actor who I'd like to single out for special praise. In his first ever acting role, he has carved out a performance worthy of a DeNiro, a Hopkins, a Clooney, perhaps even a Lassie. I'm talking about *the* find of the year, Bad Dog! Let's put our hands together for Bad Dog and wish him all the best when he wins the Oscar next month!"

Oh stop. You're making me blush.

CHAPTER 10

AND THE WINNER IS...

But Filch had been right. Not long after the premiere of *Cake Fear*, I was in line to win the best thing an actor can win: an Oscar! And with the theme of this year's Oscar ceremony being "Cuddly Protected Animals", everyone felt that I was in line to get my paws on one.

But before we get to What Happened on Oscar Night, let's quickly look in on what happened yesterday...

(Screen goes wobbly and "back in time" music comes on.)

That morning at Vince's there had been a special delivery for me. It was a parcel. A very heavy parcel. I opened it and found myself face-to-face with a gravestone.

My gravestone.

There was an inscription in gold letters carved on the front. "Bad Dog RIP" and then some dates. I knew the dates on the stone. One was my birthdate. The other was the day I was due to die. Tomorrow. The day of the Oscars. There was a note attached: "Thinking of you always," it read.

It wasn't signed, but that didn't matter. There was only one person this could be from. Hayley Froob. Raoul always had it in for me, but I'd bet every bone I'd ever buried that this was the handiwork of Froob, not DeCinque. This was different. Nastier. I showed it to Vince but he didn't get it. "Some sicko, kid," he shrugged. "Hollywood's full of 'em. Don't worry about it. I'll have a word with Sandy."

Oh, great. Sandy. My bodyguard. About as useful as a chocolate coffee-pot.

And Sandy was right alongside me as we arrived at the ceremony.

"Hi there, folks! I'm Preston Clouds! We're coming to you live from this year's Oscar ceremony! And with this year's theme being adorable little animals, here's one feller who's hoping that he can be up on that rostrum pretty soon: star of *Cake Fear,* it's Bad Dog! Bad Dog, how do you rate your chances?"

I adjusted my Vuarnet shades and gave Preston Clouds' groin a quick sniff.

"Well, Preston," I said, "since you don't understand a word I'm saying, I'd just like to say that you need to change your underwear more often. Now, if you don't mind, I'd like to get inside quick 'cos there's a loopy actress stalking me."

I hurried nervously past the rest of the press pack into the plush, air-conditioned madness of the Oscar ceremony. I slipped into my seat between Nick Jackolson and an actress called Gwyneth something.

"I like your work, man," drawled Jackolson, flashing the famous wolflike grin. "Very … nice."

"I feel, like soooo much love coming from you all … I'd like to thank my great-great-grandfather who can't be here tonight … sob!" said Gwyneth, puzzling me a bit until I realized she was practising her Oscar acceptance speech.

I looked around the rest of the audience. There was Anvil just behind me, and Vince four rows back. He gave me the thumbs up and then made a praying action with his hands. Raoul wasn't important enough to get an invite. Another thing he had against me.

Up on stage were several cages with dimly-lit animals in them. They were too far away for me to make out what kind of animals, but judging by the theme of the evening I figured the cages held some rare animal species.

As I looked around, a metallic flash from behind me, somewhere to my left, caught my super-doggy sight and I took a closer look. It was Hayley Froob, and the flash was the light catching the metal mouth brace she still wore after the explosion. My heart lurched.

She seemed very calm. She was talking to the guy next to her but she kept glancing over in my direction.

My mind skipped three gears and went straight into overdrive. What *was* she planning? Did she have a gun? A bomb? A team of deadly ninjas trained to abseil down from the roof and attack dogs? How could I defend myself? Surely she wouldn't do anything in front of this audience and with almost a billion people watching on TV?

Would she?

I heard my name and looked at the stage. Leonardo Someone or other was announcing the next Oscar category: Best Supporting Actor. "And the nominations are…" The screen behind Leo started showing clips featuring the nominated actors. I could feel Hayley Froob's eyes hot on the back of my neck. *Cake Fear* came up and there I was in a quick compilation of clips. Me licking Anvil's face. Me dragging the bomb. I risked a quick look round at Froob and saw her flinch at that bit. Back on screen I was being kidnapped.

Then a bit more of me being cute. The screen went black. There was a ripple of applause. Then an excited hush fell over the audience. Leo picked up a gold envelope and ripped it open. He looked at it, then turned to the audience.

"And the winner is ... *Bad Dog!*"

I felt my legs, all four of 'em, go wobbly as the audience erupted. Nick Jackolson pushed me into the aisle. "Go on, kid," he smiled. "Go get 'em!"

"I feel your love," sobbed Gwyneth.

This was it. Hayley Froob was certain to finish me now while she had a clear shot. I walked slowly towards the stage. In my imagination I could see Froob standing and taking aim, or pressing the remote-control detonator, or whatever other fiendish end she had planned for me.

Somehow I made it up on stage where Leo handed me the gold statue. I risked a quick look at Froob. To my surprise, instead of the gun-toting weirdo I expected to see, Froob was just sitting there, looking at me. She did have an odd expression on her face which didn't make me feel any better. She looked like she knew something I didn't.

"C'mon, BD," said Leo. "Give the folks a speech."

I stepped to the mike and cleared my throat. "Thank you," I said. "I…"

I stopped talking. Hayley Froob was grinning now and pointing past my right shoulder. I turned and followed the direction of her finger.

Behind me lay the rare-animal cages. I hadn't noticed them on the way up on to the stage. Now, closer up I noticed the dark shapes inside for the first time. There was something I didn't like about them.

"My agent always told me," quipped Leo behind me, "never work with animals, and now here I am with Bad Dog and the last two Lesser Spotted Alaskan Snow Cats in the world."

I stiffened. *Cats?* Did he say *cats?* So that was why Hayley Froob hadn't bothered to try and finish me. She knew that I would finish myself.

I couldn't help it.

I'm a dog.

They were cats.

It was a done deal.

I flung my Oscar at Leo and leaped at the cage. It spilled over and the last two remaining Lesser Spotted Alaskan Snow Cats jumped out like two ... well, cats.

They looked at me and started hissing. I looked at them. I looked at the audience and saw Vince. He was holding his hands out, palms up, and waving them from side to side in a "please don't do what you are about to do" gesture. The audience watched in horrified silence. I could see the light blinking on top of the TV camera.

"Don't do it, BD," said Leo, who, realizing what was about to go down, had put himself between me and the cats.

"Step aside, Fringe Face, if you know what's good for you," I snarled.

The red mist came down and with a roar I barged Leo out of the way. The last two Lesser Spotted Alaskan Snow Cats in the world scooted towards the back of the stage, followed by me going about two hundred miles an hour.

Watched by a TV audience of a billion, I chased the cats up and down the scenery. A large backdrop fell away, exposing the backstage area filled with cables and equipment. The door to the loading bay was open and I could see the busy street outside. The cats scooted through the door and shot out into the street, followed by me.

There was a loud squeal of brakes and tyres and then a dull thud. I skidded to a halt and peered around the door. It wasn't a pretty sight. Behind me the audience gasped as I slowly became aware of where I was and what I had just done. I had just polished off the last two Lesser Spotted Alaskan Snow Cats in the world, live on global television.

I stood and looked at the audience sitting in shocked, icy silence.

Vince had his head in his hands. In a sea of angry faces there was only one smiling face. Hayley Froob. She could hardly control her tears of laughter. The people in the seats next to her thought she was crying and tried to comfort her.

I held up my paws and tried to think of something to say.

"Whoops?"

Leonardo walked up rubbing his head where my Oscar had pinged him. Immediately the atmosphere inside the auditorium turned nasty. Very nasty indeed. Really famous movie stars fought with each other for the chance to get their hands on me.

Expensive designer ball-gowns were ripped to pieces as actresses stormed the stage, eyes bulging. Many of them were using very rude words. They were all super-fit as well. Fast runners. Big muscles.

Despite the condition of the actors, Vince was actually the first to get near me. He had hastily written a legal document on the back of a paper napkin which basically said that he was no longer my agent and was not responsible for anything I did or had done, now or at any time in the past on this planet or any planets yet to be discovered. And he could keep any money I had earned or would ever earn in the movies. Quick work. "Sign here, kid," he puffed. "No offence, but I can't have anything to do with you any more. Bye." He had always been a big softy, Vince.

I slapped my paw mark on the "contract" and Vince legged it. Behind him the stampede was almost on me.

There was no time to waste, so I shot out of the loading-bay doors and, taking care not to make the same mistake as the Lesser Spotted Alaskan Snow Cats, I waited for a break in the traffic. In fact there were plenty of breaks 'cos the traffic was snarled up rubbernecking the remains of the accident.

The tuxedoed and sequinned mob wasn't far behind and I ducked into an alleyway. It was filled with dumpsters and rotting cars. It was also a dead end. I backed up, looking for a way out. The ground trembled as the A-list actors and actresses scented blood. My blood.

It looked like this was it.

"Pssst!" said a pile of garbage next to me.

I nearly jumped out of my skin.

"In here, son," it said, opening the lid on a dumpster. "You don't want that bunch getting their hands on you. Trust me, I know what I'm talking about."

I didn't have time to think about it and leaped into the rotting filth inside. Almost immediately I heard the chasing mob hurtling down the alley. I was sure I could hear Antonio Banderas and Brad Pitt arguing about which of them was going to throttle me. "I swear on the life of my unborn sons I will teach that cur some manners and avenge the honour of my father!" said Banderas, getting things a bit mixed up, I felt.

"I'm sure that little scumbag went this way," said someone who sounded like Julia Roberts. "Pass me that baseball bat, Bullock."

I hunkered deeper into the dumpster. These guys really wanted to do some damage.

"Affleck, Stiller, you seen anythin'?"

"No, Sly, not a thing."

Gradually the voices started to move back down the alley.

"C'mon, everyone," said Madonna, or someone who sounded just like her, "he's given us the slip. Let's get back inside and trash the place!"

After a few minutes all I could hear was the rumble of traffic from the street. The lid of the dumpster flipped open and the pile of garbage who had saved my life looked in. "OK, they've gone. You can get out now," it said.

I clambered out. Now that I had a chance to look, I could see that underneath the grime and garbage was a dog. A big, shaggy hound. There was something very familiar about his face.

"You recognize me?" he said. "The name's..."

"Mozart!" I yelled. "You're Mozart, from that dog movie!"

"That's right," said Mozart. "I was a dog star too. For a while. I recognized you straight away – you're that Bad Dog guy, right? I saw what happened in the street. That was you chasing those cats?"

I nodded.

"They love ya for being a dog on the screen," said Mozart sadly. "Then when you actually act like a real dog you get the treatment. You end up ... here."

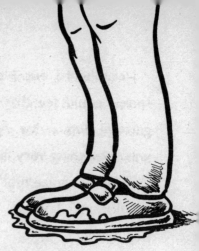

"What happened to you?" I said.

"Took a leak on Spielberg's favourite suede shoes. He seemed OK about it, but everything sort of stopped after that. The phone stopped ringin', you know? The offers dried up. I did a few TV commercials, then I was down to opening supermarkets, that sort of thing. Then eventually, nothing. I got canned by my agent and here I am."

He picked a piece of burger off his shoulder and munched it thoughtfully. "If I was you I'd keep your head down for a while. Find somewhere real quiet. Somewhere you can rest up and get your act back together."

I knew just the place. I thanked Mozart and trudged out into the city night. There was only one place in the city that I really knew where I'd be welcome. Somewhere where I could at least get a bed and some food. And only one person I knew in Hollywood who understood me.

Anvil Studminder.

But before I made it over to Anvil's pad, I got snatched by the City Dog Catcher and ended up back in Z-Block.

So much for the plan.

CHAPTER 11

BACK IN THE JUG AGAIN

So. Here we are again.

That's about all there is to tell.

Everything was about the same as before. Fester had watched the whole thing on TV and had kept my old cell ready for me.

"That was some act, 'Boomerang'," he laughed. "You really screwed things up for yerself, ya dumb mutt. 'Boomerang'," he said again, jabbing me with his broom. "Get it? On account of how you jes'